THIS WALKER BOOK BELONGS TO:

_____

_____

_____

_____

I
CAN'T
SLEEP

For Sophie

First published 1990 by
Walker Books Ltd, 87 Vauxhall Walk
London SE11 5HJ

This edition published 1992

© 1990 Philippe Dupasquier

Printed and bound in Hong Kong by
South China Printing Co. (1988) Ltd

British Library Cataloguing in Publication Data
Dupasquier, Philippe
I can't sleep.
I. Title
823 [J]
ISBN 0-7445-2061-4

I CAN'T SLEEP

Philippe Dupasquier

WALKER BOOKS
LONDON

MORE WALKER PAPERBACKS
For You to Enjoy

Also by Philippe Dupasquier

·BUSY PLACES

Six books full of machines and activity. From page to page the scenery stays the same,
but various people come and go and a number of different stories unfold.

"The balance of continuity and change is beautifully even, the illustrations are bright, full of detail but never confusing, and the books are, above all, fun." *British Book News*

The Railway Station   0-7445-0977-7   *The Factory*   0-7445-0978-5
The Harbour   0-7445-0979-3   *The Garage*   0-7445-0937-8
The Airport   0-7445-0938-6   *The Building Site*   0-7445-0939-4
£2.99 each

THE GREAT ESCAPE

A prisoner is chased by a gang of warders in this classic wordless picture book.

"Brilliant and breathless… Each scene is packed with comic detail." *The Times Literary Supplement*

ISBN 0-7445-1365-0   £3.99